The
Red
Shoes
New

The Red Shoes New

BIN SOBCHUK

iUniverse®

THE RED SHOES NEW

iUniverse books may be ordered through booksellers or by contacting:

iUniverse
1663 Liberty Drive
Bloomington, IN 47403
www.iuniverse.com
1-800-Authors (1-800-288-4677)

ISBN: 978-1-4917-9095-3 (sc)
ISBN: 978-1-4917-9092-2 (e)

Library of Congress Control Number: 2016904839

Print information available on the last page.

iUniverse rev. date: 04/06/2016

Contents

1

The Red Shoes

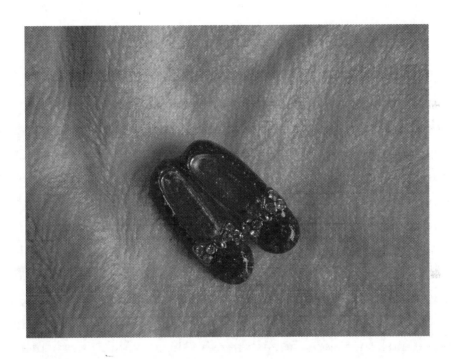

Another day begins. When Margret wakes up, it is already noon. No one will blame her, as she has already separated from her husband over 2 years. The medications for her mental illness knock her down for years. Yet she still feels O.K. now. At least she is not worried about her family's finances too much. During the marriage, she really needed to work very hard to make ends meet. Her husband is a playboy. There were several things on her mind she needed to buy, so she decides to go to the shopping mall near her home. She put on a simple skirt without bra, and wore a pair of red slipper shoes just like at home. She goes.

On the street, cars are busy, rushing from place to place. Peter, a policeman in the 14 Division, is in charge of this area. He likes his job. He thinks that it is a kind of power and admire for people. Friday afternoons make him more and more miss his tender wife and one lovely daughter. He prayed to finish soon. After stopped the car in front of the mall, he walks in. It is not that busy, maybe because it is an Indian summer! "Who is that?" He thought. A big woman (mildly obese) with a cart and a pair of red shoes. He notices her and carefully watch her. She is a visible minority, and looks like a Korean or Chinese with mental illness, because she is not alert all the time. Suddenly, he recalled the hell's fire. About two years ago, in the same mall, he saw an aboriginal woman. She dressed with a west style long skirt with her aboriginal traditional necklaces. She walked in the mall for a long time and restless. Her chubby face and sturdy body made her nervous. A man with jean and T-shirt came to her and talked to her. She looked so happy and went with the man. What a hell! Just over one month, Peter saw her again, but this time, it was her corpse. It was a brutal and bloody nasty murder. She died for long time tortured and dismembered body. Peter never forgot her cut off forelegs. He blamed himself over and over again. "Why I did not stop them at the first place! Why I did not catch it?" she died forever, but not in Peter's mind. I will never forget 80% rate homicide women who are killed by her boyfriend, husband, common-law husband … I should do something. I will …

Margret walks in the mall. On the one hand, she thinks what she should buy, on the other hands, she watch the customers in the mall. She likes it-urban, luxury and adultery. She did not notice that someone has already spied on her and protect her on the spot. "Electronic Store" she stops. She is a regular customer here. The customer services immediately recognize her and service her. Talk and choose a headphone. Peter on the other side bows to point to goods right in front of Margret. She noticed him so close to see his uniform-three national flags-one on chest-two on both shoulders. She saw his face, not a blonde. He looks at Margret sometimes. She begins to think whether or not he wants to further contact? Nevertheless she does not like to go toward to him; it is not her style. She knows her eyes are her weapons. She watches him and waits for his coming. For a while, he used polices' secret language-nose to answer her. He refused. She did not care, and pulled her cart going away. Who cares about the black boots! As many people know, her ex-husband is much more handsome than him. He has overestimated himself. She continues to go to General-Merchandise and get what she wanted. When she comes back, passing this store again, one employee faced her doing Eskimo kiss. She passes with a glance.

Soon she is back home. She recalls the policeman. In her simple mind, she regrets that she should dress up and wear a pair of fashion shoes and walk to him. No, No, No. I am a religious woman. I go to church on Sundays. How I can let a police walk into me so indecently. My ex-husband is so tall and white and blue eyes. I cannot accept others' invasion. Love in the church is so wonderful. She never forget church's single party. They met and he invited her to dance and they were the first couple to dance in the whole party. She revelled in the perfect moment until now. No bell rings in our church. We are different. She suddenly stands up and watches the mirror. How sad it is. She is not just like before. She gained a lot of weight. After married, he quit his job and totally relied on her income. She had to work very hard to make a living. She was sick many times and is much fatter. She never goes to the party besides churches'. She is afraid of being unpopular or giggling. There are no children even though they married a couple of years ago. Her tears had already gone. She did not cry since she was a kid. God's almighty makes her believe in Him. Yet after marrying, she lost.

Peter finished patrolling the mall. He is off and goes directly home. His lovely daughter first smiles and then kisses him. His beloved wife is cooking. He is happy today. He knows he did the right thing and let a woman become a happy lady. After long long time bloody murder shadow now has a glimpse of sunshine.

2

Transsexual

Toronto's best strip club is south of the intersection of Yonge Street and Bloor Street. Sometimes, I go there for fun. They have some transsexuals and many female strip dancers. One shemale deeply impressed me. I am her big fan. (I will call him she for respect.)

She wore a pure white and transparent cloak to dance. This cloak made her invisible to people. She danced but never smiled. Her body shape was not perfect like "V," but she was woman's middle size-not too big or too small. She was good at pole dancing. After the DJ announced her and after the applause, she began to take off her dresses. She had small boobs. Her belly was almost flat. When she put down her underwear to play, I saw her male sexual organ was removed. Her big brother sat in front of the stage. He cheered her and encouraged her. That was a painful story.

She was a he, an unknown poor guy. He worked hard but just could survive. He dreamed to change his fate. He was eager to be rich and famous in the society. One day his big brother brought him here. They saw the dance. His brother asked "Hi, buddy, can you dance like them?" He did not reply. His brother continue to say, "As a man, you are too short and your body shape is not perfect. If you want to earn some money from strip dance, you need to be a transsexual." He was surprised. "How much?" he hesitated. "A lot, my buddy, besides if you succeed, you are famous too. That is your dream, right?" He went home. He almost could not believe it. Too much conflict. He took off his clothes; stood in front of mirror watching his ambition's part. "I am over 20 years old, but I have no girlfriend, no sex even. ***I am Mr. Nobody!*** I know I can dance. I learned ballet when I was young, yet I also wish I had a normal life – a family … which one is more important?" he thought. One week past, his big brother called him "Are you all right? Still do the manual labour? Time does not come back!" This time his big brother took him to the stage. Let a coach teach him how to dance. It was good. He looked up the stage and imaged audience and being rich. He agreed to it. "Yes, that is my dream!" Before the operation, his big brother went with him to the best brothel for his farewell bachelor party. Then the operation was painful but not too bad. Soon she is a new star of this strip club. Now, she has money, friends, and followers. She feel that she has succeeded.

Most audiences come at night. She is a little bit shy to face hundreds of people. She also feel reluctant to show her private parts. On the stage, she had done her best. After that, she deeply thought, "Where I belong?" One night, she had a dream: she saw a lot of transsexuals crossing a huge tropical jungle. While they are walking, sometimes they saw transsexuals living in the jungle. After they finally go to the other side of the jungle, they reunite there. They celebrate there. They do not experience that they are not perfect; meanwhile, they appreciate each other and love their new looks and bodies very much. Some of them take life mates and continue to go further with pleasure; some live there; some return back to the starting point. The returning ones face the "normal" people, nevertheless their hearts do not belong here anymore. She had no place to hide. She showed her scars every day. She even felt that she was not a human being. She did not visit her parents for years, because she did not want to hurt them. Her big brother came often. He treated her good but strictly. He warned her "You cannot dance for the whole life; earning money is most important for you."

She used pure white and transparent cloak to hide herself on the stage, which displayed her fragile inside. She wished that she could never go back to the strip club and instead vanish into the jungle. "Call me shemale."

3

New Hope

US President Barack Obama's famous graffiti is a classic pose- raising arm salute. I saw it many times. I do not know whether he post it in order to raise a race or to rule the whole world. Four years ago, he did kill some terrorists, who he believed were dangerous. Obviously, the black and the African mix-blooded view the president Obama as a successful role model. They broke the barriers with all nations; furthermore they are very proud of their heritage.

In Canada, I saw Muslims undergoing struggle; I saw the economics of oriental nations booming; I also saw numerous African try to let the whole world remember the turning point epoch. Let's look at Africa; their fatherland. Did the president help them and make many countries better and better? Does he really want to do so? In history, if you try to let people remember you longer, the easiest way is to kill. Conquering the Middle East reveals the American dream, which has already destroyed many countries. In "us" History, many presidents already did so; President Obama is not the first one to show his ambitions by this way; may not be the last one to do it either.

When I studied in college, I dreamt of going to Africa to work; to help the needy. Now I am in North America; I can see the different peoples from the whole world. I receive more than I give. I appreciate it so much.

As a President of USA, leading a race had better be winning by peace, not by revenge.

4

Party Money

In our home, there are four big book shelves on one side of the wall. Besides books, we have some fun stuffs there. One blue pottery pot had "Party Money" printed on it. This pot has a long story. My boyfriend George' father gave it to him when he was in high school.

George was born in a middle class family. His father was a very intelligent worker; he often created a lot of tools. Yet life was tough; he needed to save money and also taught George to do the same things. Before his high school, just the richest students could hold birthday parties and they also invited their richest friends too. Unfortunately, nobody invited George, even once! He felt a little bit sad. In high school, he became socialized. He fell in love a girl whose name is Jones. He really wanted to be invited to her birthday party. He tried to save money. George' father gave him lunch money, but he often ran home to eat to save a quarter. He worked summer jobs. One day he thought that it was a good time to show his affection; he asked her whether or not he could attend her birthday party? Jones was surprised. George said that "I have money; I will give you the best birthday gift!" She refused him. This time, he was really hurt then went home silently. He told mom about it. Finally his dad knew about it too. The other day, dad bought a pottery pot with "Party Money" printed on it, putting on his book shelf. He told dad, "I like it."

Now this pottery pot is in front of my books. I have a story too. I was born and grew up in China. First we did not have this culture to hold parties for children. I first knew birthday parties when I was 15 years old, about 1990's. Secondly, I am not popular at all. No one will invite me to his or her parties, even my cousins. They are younger than me and richer and popular. I do not mind them. I like reading. I always go to book stores. I own a lot of books. That is my party money. I remember I studied until midnight; occasionally, I watched stars sparkle in the blue sky; I knew that one day I will be something!

5

Jack and Shy Girl

Lisa: Hi Jack, how did you tell your wife that you are willing to be spanked? I cannot tell my husband that secret of mine. Yet I truly want it …

Jack: "Hi shy girl, I started spanking my girlfriends when I was in High School. I did not want to do it but I was in love with a very strong domineering female. My mother had just spanked me and she blistered my bottom well then just after that spanking my girlfriend slapped me for no reason and I told her the next time she's getting a spanking. She did it and I spanked her in a car parked along a dirt road in the woods. A few weeks later she wanted me to do it again."

"I was spanking my wife for about 15 years when the thought occurred to me that she should be doing some of the spanking too. Suggest it to him in a sweet way; pat his bottom in a loving way with "bad boy," coming from you he may be showing you some encouraging signs. I don't know him but I would suggest not dominating him or being demanding about what you want, Play-Play-Play, give him time to find his way to your lap. Real spankings will develop once he is secure emotionally with you and him where you want to put him with your hairbrush in hand and his bare ass up on your lap."

"The first bare bottom spanking my wife gave me was almost unbearable, but it felt proper, as she was doing it, it felt like she was the only one that could get-a-way with this and she did and so can you; no one knows your husband better than you. I think you know how to get your way with him and I would be the last guy to bet against a woman that wanted something and could not get what she wanted from a guy. Never seen that yet! If you want it you will be spanking him-you'll figure it out. It will be the best thing for the both of you. My wife and I talk about spanking and there was a time she could not say the word, "spanking" When she says it I listen!"

Lisa:

I was born and taught in Mainland China. My father was a senior professor and dean in the biggest university of China. Most of his students are pursuing doctor's degree. My mother was an engineer who worked in a national defence institute. She does not love me too much and abused me both in physically and emotionally. Sometimes I wish that the whole world just left two persons-my Father and -me. I was certainly punished by him too.

I was married to my husband over four years. He is a white Canadian. Like my family, his mother was a high school principle and graduated from the best university of Canada. Being spanked by my parents is my secret; willing by Him is my taboo. Sleeping in bed, we dream the difference. His Shining skin makes me revel. It is my first time that I forget my parents. Calm-Calm-Calm, he finally fell to sleep. Tears down I know I am his wife.

Your email has shocked me. I just realized what the difference between punishment and sexual abuse is. I never stop thinking what I want. For the past few nights, I experienced frequently untouchable sexual sensation; same to you. Which one is first? Physical or Emotional? Should we finish this stupid game and pretend to be normal? Keep our Hollywood's unforgettable.

Jack:

"It is not about abuse, it's reasonable and the wording is much more than the reality with my wife and me and the other women that I have had the pleasure and good luck to spank and a few spanked me. It's not reality. Abuse is wrong and the last thing my wife or I would do. Somehow for us, playing is more fun than physical pain. I would never hurt a woman and have never been harmed by the ladies I talk about; it's play. I've never spanked a child and never would. I've spanked mothers that wanted spanking in a special way. I do not hurt women and no one should! This is at a higher level for me, it's about playing that we don't do as adults so why be adults all the time-it sucks. No one has the right or should ever consider hurting another emotionally or physically. Playing with the wording is one thing but the really is different-be respectful and careful, always. She is always in charged."

"It was hard for my wife to spank me but now we spank each other. We have been spanking for a very long time so this is easy for us. We spank for pleasure and for pain and we know how to do both depending on the circumstances and needs of each. When I've been bad she is like my mother was with me and I feel very much like a boy getting a spanking from an adult woman. Her spankings can be very pleasurable or extremely painful. I'm a situation with her now. Last week I had a bad day at work and that evening I was drinking too much wine and got drunk and started cussing and directed a few of those words towards her. I saw that expression in her face and I got scared, nervous and my knees felt like Jell-O when she said, "You're getting a good hard spanking for this and them I'm going to whip your spanked ass even more with my strap." She tried to do it a week ago Saturday but I interfered, I'm stalling. I love her play spankings but when she is like a mother spanking me like a son-she is like my Mother spanking me to tears."

"Sometimes I'm crying when she has me bare ass up across her lap getting her spanking brush that is causing my bottom to change from a burning sensation to blazing sensations because I was bad she is setting my ass on fire with her spanking brush, she is very good at doing this. We love each other and there is nothing that seems abusive about it I love having my wife as my disciplinarian. It feels and seems very proper- a woman that knows how to give me spanking me like a boy and sometimes I'm crying about it, and that feels good too."

"Would you like to do this with your husband, spank him like a boy? Once you start spanking it gets easier and the intensity increases with each spanking. If he agrees you will learn how to control him while you are spanking him. I know plenty of women that are spanking men, husbands and others and making a guy's cry is something they all like to do, maybe you would too, it's not that hard to do once you start spanking for a reason. I know guys that have wives that are spanking them and us all feel very lucky. But I enjoy spanking women too."

Lisa:

Spanking for fun is pleasure. Yet my husband does not have this hobby. Countable intercourse for me is suffered. Nothing to shed; No more please. The man could rule you and conquer your heart. "I want a kid," I begged him. Ironically, after one year we married, the doctor said that, "he has no sperms." From then on, he is just a boy in my mind. I am not a mother either. We do have real life spanking once. He likes playing on line games. Once, I truly could not tolerate it anymore. I gave him a stroke. He stop the game; "Sweetie what do you want?" shocked me. This time, he played with me but not what I want. Attempting with others like our group is fantastic. Couldn't stop watching and learning. Switch is reality.

Jack's writing is quotation.

6

Brian Parsons and I

Toronto spanking club is amazing. People in this club find what they used to mistreat or eager to be a dominant. Two years ago, I finally joined the club. I searched on-line a lot of spanking movies and videos. I began to know that I am not the only crazy one who want to be a spanker or spankee. We have a yahoo messenger; there I met a lot of fans. Brian is one. The first night crash was truly unforgettable. He and I chat with typing, so smooth. My humour and wisdom gave him a deep impression. In the meanwhile, his thoughtfulness brought warm and tender to me. That night he said that he wish he was in Toronto. (He was in PA). He also made fun of me. He said that he would come to Toronto for **Date** soon. We used language and icons to spank each other and enjoyed the responds. Both of us spanked to pants down. Until now I still remember his lessons. Almost 2 am we had to finish our conversations. After a few days, I printed what we typed that night. I waited him several nights, but no results. I even sent many emails to him, yet no reply either. I thought that I lost him.

Time flees so fast. Last week, I went to yahoo messenger; to be surprised I found that he was there. I directly said, "Family guy"! (His nickname) He forgot me. I was so hurt but I gave him many hints to try to let him recall me. Finally, he knew who I am. Both of us chat for fun again. Old friends are always better. He is witty and uses my sentences against me. This time I asked him for pictures. He sent me 3 pictures; one of them is spanking one. He is muscle; I like it.

He was spoiled when he was young. He said that his parents never spanked him. He even pretended to make mistakes and let his parents spank him, but they would not. At this point, he is a sunshine boy! I am a shady girl. I love his English teaching. He do improve my English, but also fine me. It is a wonderful sensation for both of us. I do not know how far from Toronto to PA; I wish that I could drive there to see him for curious, and for our holy purposes. God blessed us. Today I went to yahoo messenger; I see him again! Yet he has no respond. But I still tangle what we talked before and try to image his face and the whole body. (He did not send a picture with his face.) What do I expect! I am already satisfied. One person cares me not far from me; for me it is enough. (Compared with my whole families live in China) I know I cannot live in USA for years since I get ODSP in Canada. If I live in USA, I cannot get money from the government. I wait one day, I visit him or he comes to Toronto.

Thank Toronto spanking club. We can meet and be friends. Keep in touch!
On-line spanking

7

Corner Time — Good Morning Mama

I am not the first boy in my family. Every morning I enjoy a kiss from my beloved Mom, who also provides food to me. Soon, my siblings get the contributions as same as mine. I hate this daily routes. As a Muslim, I have chosen today to show my ambitions. Not because of scores, or love or jealousy; my corner where I stood, she knew. Her hands were square and spanked fast. I did not understand her corrections just to firm my butt. She was more angry, "mauve, mauve, I am not blind!" "Cane me first." I ordered. We did have a cane in our room. Mom put down my trousers, I looked back as normal. "Put on my son." she said. I immediately took off my underwear. First cane I had, was not straight. I slightly bent over. Mom still there. How come?

She is not a nominal. I had to tell her, "Last Friday I got seven paddle from the priest." She calmed down. This time I swallowed no. Eight. I was not surprised, my ass already down to the bottom. I did not know how I can say stop or put my own clothes on. I dared to look back. Mom knew. She saw my butt black and blue; she slowly put on my clothes. This time she said "Salute!"

8

My Kitty- Prince

Prince is the first kitty that I am bringing up. Now he is 10 months old. He is my son. I still remember that when I just adopted him, he was small and lean. So every time, I did grocery shopping, I saved some money and bought all kinds of kitty food for him. Once, I saved one dollar, I bought a big seafood can for him. He liked it very much and ate two days! I call him prince, because he is dashing and handsome. I love his eyes, so big. Everybody who first time see him say that he has big and bright eyes!

He sometimes is very naughty. My boyfriend often chases him from dining table. Prince eats his boots' laces. He drives my boyfriend crazy! He also has a secret-he does not know how to cover his poo and pee. We suffer a lot of it. My prince is ma-ma's boy. I love him more than everything. I feed him, bath him; by the way, my boyfriend clean his cat and my prince's kitty litter boxes. It is really a nasty job.

Prince likes to play with my foot. I always move my foot and prince comes here and play with me. He liked it when he was very young. He also likes to play with my socks too. A long while, I cannot find the same pair of socks to wear! Prince has very big and bright eyes. Everybody who see him first time say so. I feel that cat's eyes are spiritual matters. Many people are afraid of it. My prince is a pure black cat. I do not believe that black cat is bad luck. I love him forever!

9

Elf Miss His Giant

"I was born to be an elf!" I always think this way. All the women like giants? *No*! My secret weapon- my –knife did kill several mistresses. My best one is a spark skinny lady with a 3 years old blonde boy. My height is a secret too, very unusual. If I squat down, I am shorter than a 3-year-old. My nice fair hair is all over me and body size saves me. Girls look back; I do not care. My goal is being a real father with no my biology child. Tidy is skinny intoxicate in herself. Elf peeked it for a while. Showing busy often is a good impression. Washroom is a best place to see my knife. 2 weeks passed. One day she waited her son then into the washroom. I grab my mop and barrow into the washroom too. I mopped the washroom out part. She seems seeing me here. "Excuse me, it is convenient …" she asked. "Sorry I think if I can clean it earlier, I can go home earlier. But if you mind, I go now." She come out with smile. "No need hurry; my home is near." I succeed! She must be a single mother; otherwise, she could not so brave.

That night three of us come to her home. There are two rooms. The kid sleep in one; we sleep with our wild dream. She seems overexcited. I already experienced this kind of life. Now we become underground couple. My bigger goal is that let her feel I am no difference with her son and I can enjoy easy life and still replace her husband. Further I have the right to behaviour her only boy-Spanking him or more. One day a chance comes. I pretended horny and make love with her in the kitchen. Good, her son saw it vividly. After that, I spanked him on my lap. I warn him "Do not do it again." I really enjoy these for months. Her home now is my home too.

"Baby, I am home now." I rush into kitchen for food. O my God! A giant man literally over 6 feet tall stare at me. My first reaction is her partner. I roll my eyes called "baby where you are?" no answer. My God I am in trouble. The giant look down upon me said: "I am her husband!" I immediately scared and try to run away. This time, it is a bad luck. He caught me and spanking me on his lap. By far, I still remember the lesson.

This is not the end. The giant found my superior and told him my love affairs and spanking his child. I scared to die. ***I will go down to jail!*** My superior smile to me "One more pants down to jail."

10

Brother Gardein

9 years ago, I first met our bishop Gardein James in the Mormon Church Toronto Ward. He is young, married and has 5 children. He is quiet, also a blonde. At that time, I was busy to study so I did not go to church regularly. One day I went to church for sacrifices meeting. He sat in the middle of the stage. After a while, his younger son was crying outside the door. He was still there and seemed that nothing happened. As a 29 years old "big" girl, mother's love suddenly took over me. I watch him for a long time. He saw me too. First time he avoided; second time, he left to see his crying son. I could not forget it. I like children too.

We notice each other for years, but seldom talk together. Last year, he released bishop position. Now our former bishop becomes a guy.

This year I went to church's picnic. My new boyfriend George did not show. Brother Gardein often stood in the centre to chat with others. Sometimes, I watched him at a distance. Once I looked at him, his one foot stepped on bench and talked with our Steak Centre president and his wife. So strange! I do not like it. I faced to another side. He saw me. He back his hands and pulled his pants and strip dance. It is Bill Clinton and Lewinsky's classics classic! My ex-husband's name is William. Our love tragedy is playboy's game. He is handsome but an ass hole! I love George - my new boyfriend.

Brother Gardein criticized me in public when he was a bishop. He is always changeable. I sat on bench. He walked toward me. He pretended to say hello to the sister beside me, then he greeted me. Right on the spot, his wife rushed into here and showed very excited to talked to the person beside me. Our conversation suddenly stopped. I was not surprised. I can understand his wife and him. After his wife had gone, he chose watermelon and Chinese food to eat. Watermelon is my favourite food. I knew that he also peeked me. He is a professional actor. He is blonde, looks good, but not tall. I guess that he does not play action movies or fighting drama. As a father of 5, he is busy. He has his nest. At this point, he is fully blessed.

11

Islam and Christianity Comparison

Every time I miss my hometown, Changchun City in China, I will recall our old mosque. It is over 2 hundred years old. It looks like the Forbidden City in Beijing. I have 2 Quran books. Sometimes I read them and compare them with the Book of Mormon and the Bible. Islam followers must pray 5 times a day. They believe that Allah knows everything so they directly get information from Allah. They do not need something in between to connect with Allah. This is the most important difference between Christianity and Islam.

If you look at a mosque, you will see the crescent moon on the top of mosque. Usually, it has crescents and five point stars on the towers. People living in moonlight have a conflict of interest. Islam shows it. On one hand, they have their brother's love; on the other hand they have fought each other for decades. Compared with the Muslim religion, Christianity has over 2.2 billion people in the whole world. By far it is the largest religion in the whole world too. Many churches claim that it is the only true church in the whole world; in the meantime, they all accept each other. By far Christianity has not had many wars yet.

Islam says: "thanks God." Christian says: "thank God." A Muslim says, "Islam is my Deen" which means that Islam is my belief and faith. Christians believe that God creates the earth and humans. Islam believes that Allah created the whole universe and knows the whole universe. If you destroy Allah, you will destroy the whole universal. Muslims participate in pilgrimage at least once in their whole life which is called Hajj. Mormon churches have temples. We should go to temples as many as possible and even marry and seal in temples. Mohammed is Allah's messenger. They also believe that Jesus is Allah's messenger too.

Muslims like to be clean during prayer. They wash before they pray. They clean the floor wherever it is dirty. They wash fruits before they eat them. They brush teeth whenever they can. Every time I see Muslim women veiled; I feel their purity, glory, dignity, and space. How did a person with a different belief marry a Muslim lady? I know many Muslim men whose mothers do have many children. Muslim men give their love and Manhood to their wives and children. Jesus Christ also taught us mercy and belief. No matter what, both Christianity and the Islamic religion pray peace and love upon everybody.

12

My Correction

I am innocent, but police sent me to jail. One correction broke into my heart. I do not know how they know that I can write well. Jail does give us paper and pencil every day. First day, I had a dream, which regards a little elephant. When I wake up, I still remember it vividly. I do not know where I got this thought. I just wrote down it exactly what the dream was or say word by word.

In the daytime, the correction officer saw me and looked like he was surprised. When he handcuffed me, I saw his tattoo. The right arm was a bald eagle; the left arm was a skeleton and a big sailing boat. I was surprised too! I thought to myself, about the correction officer, "You are a bald eagle?" No matter what Canadian always says, if America is a bald eagle, we are a baby eagle. My challenge obviously touched him. This is our first real sight.

On my first day, my hearing failed because I was missing a few documents. Yet for the whole day, Miss Thomson and I were locked in the same cell. Her unusual performance gave me a deep impression. I called her "my Tommy." Then that day I did feel that I am so lucky that I took the same truck with her back to jail too. On the road, I could see she was very near. She never told to me or faced me, but I could see her lifestyle, her facial expression and her habits. My head was full of her now. I tried to remember all kinds of information during the whole day. After eating, I grabbed a pencil and paper and rushed into my own cell. Almost without thinking, I sat and wrote my essay "My Tommy ." Soon I finished it. I read and corrected some places, and then I fell asleep.

The second morning, I dropped my essay for corrections. I went to the dining room to have breakfast. He-My correction officer jumped into my sight. He opened his legs towards the woman correction after saw me. I immediately felt aggressive. I rolled my eyes. He was serious and squatted to write down some notes. Next, he handcuffed everybody again. When he did it to me, I saw his long, long, fair hair covering the tattoo. It is beautiful. I recalled my husband's arms. The same fair colour hair on his arms and body too. I suddenly felt that maybe I cannot see him anymore. He also watched me so as to forget I am not the last one to be handcuffed. There was one more after me. I heard women correction officers were giggling. Never mind. Finally, he raised his thumb and said, "Perfect." My heart pumped hard; my face turned red. I knew that I made a big impression on him. I was in conflict. I could not compete with him in this situation, yet he made it happen. He gave me more than that-it is hope, desire, fairness and love …

After that, I went to the police truck. When we went to College Park, another favour happened. He first asked the police to do me a favour; let my case go first. Then he knew that my case was on at 3 o'clock, he even got angry with the police. He left. Finally, my case finished at 11 o'clock. I knew that it was because of his efforts. I was free now. My social worker gave me one bus token to home. I went home; I was sick and very confused. Yet I never forgot him; his appreciation and his love encouraged me to continue my writing and studies.

Now my husband has separated from me over 2 years. His fair hair flirt me to recall my correction over and over again. Now when I think of my correction officer's tattoo. The bald eagle is not just him; it is me; it is us free from jail.

I must say that sometimes I am bored. I looked back on the police many times. But I do not fear. I miss my correction officer. I knew that he give me more than the police. Sometimes I am horny. I do want to hook up with them. Every time I think so, I miss him double or triple …

I am not a jail bird.

13

Dirty Monkey-Master Piece

Today is interesting, in deed. Two male masters discipline the whole gym classes. One likes ballerina; one is "dirty monkey."

Who likes fast-bastard? Never heard of it from an instructor! Male dominate classes may be undergoing. Yet female doggies are not easy to hook up with. Just experiencing Olympic Games, I see higher, faster, and stronger. Life is so true, the monkey has bigger ears and Mongols-like head. Hopefully the bird also works out. He taught me with body languages more. I am not a fast learner, my chest pressed the mattress; my arms are weak; which made me cannot move too much.

Learning is amazing. Shy means you cannot do it. Try is first step. Try my best means that I might be the last one. I do not believe a professional coach is so moved. Not this time.

In his classes, he often mentions police: how they pick up a man to a fit his career. Interesting, this is my concern too. Some methods are challenging for me-inferior. He also taught us how to fight. I am an amateur now! I know this is my last choice. I should not fight with anybody, especially police. No pain no gain. I lose my body weight and know others' secrets. Although this is not a lab, some people's bodies are master pieces. In my age, I prefer power yet I am not rich to reach it to proof I can!

If a police cadet wrote down in his training notes: full of pain, I know why they strike for more than they deserve. They just have 3 months training and become a "super hero." Girls like them. For me, in college I did not like them. It was hard to meet them at all. I lose my chance to be a professional lady by far. Low social esteem, I have disability too. My goal is: look good and feel good.

Do you feel opposite sex is trouble? I even can get their body cologne smell. Dirty monkey even alerted me that my breast will down to knees!

Note: wear bra. My husband did say so. Love conquered all.

14

Dirty Monkey 2

Today I chose dirty monkey's class. He taught us with a good speed, which made me catch up with. One skip game is still my weakness. I cannot follow it. He said bastard again. Suddenly, I really feel I am stupid. He taught me one on one many times; I appreciate. His giant ears are useful. He can hear us murmurs. His eye bones are protruding; big eyes; monkey face.

My body shape totally destroyed me. The tummy is as big as a bear's. I dreamed that one day, I lose weight, I will …

He can read woman's mind. Today, he taught us a pose from Marilyn Monroe-gay icon- Beautiful and sexist. I never dream that will happen in my life. Truly, a person can change others; also can change other people's world.

Famous old Chinese proverb: Heroes love countries yet more love beauties. Who would like to give up the hottest and cutesy one to your opposite? Who cares whether tomorrow will come or not; who cares how long romance will last? I do not have confidence to do so; however dirty monkey has already worked it out.

I do not remember how many times I pretend to love ones and make love with them. I as a human being should choose from a natural one to a holy one. Always choose right, It is time to behave myself.

15

My Views on the Independence of Tibet

Tibet 2,000 years ago, on two occasions with the Chinese Han Dynasty and the pro; and set the inscription belongs to China. These two pro made a great contribution to productivity in Tibet, Tibet has two religious leaders. However, since I have memory from the da Lai Lama is the sworn enemy of the Communist Party of China has never been positive publicity.

As a Chinese citizen the right to 29 years, there still are no rights to vote. Do not know where the Chinese Communist Party's human rights. Primary school to university to study hard, actively explore and easily slack. Communist Party of China is an extreme manifestation of education in me. I notoriety from a girl to a "dog bites man," so I see the shortcomings of education in China.

In 2002, I harbored the worship of the North American civilization came to Canada 10 years of experience has taught me to see what is called democracy, independent! Tibet is not very understanding of the Tibetan people's own unique religious, devout, and their bodies are different from ours I feel - that Tibet is a Tibetan indigenous people of Tibet Communist Party seems to respect Tibetan religion, but to use their education to talented people so many local people to re-consider where to go. This is not equal, nor are human rights. Tibetan people love their own culture does not adequately reflect the independence of Tibet is an independent Tibetan culture, is the continuation of the Tibetan civilization of the Tibetan people should right to vote, every four years and choose to stay the decision.

16

The Little Man's Breakfast

People often feel that the taller a guy is the more handsome. Yet I have my own magnificent plan. Firstly, I need to eliminate same sex demean. Secondly, I want to attract some powerful opposite sex. Unfortunately, I am just a little man – no complicated background; no money. In man's world, I try to work hard and smart. My third job is as a General- Merchandise package clerk. It made me stupid. Not only could I not reach the top of the shelf, but also short of strength. My colleagues who worked with me laughed at me; even the most normal clerk though that. He is a superman, compared with me. My poor heart is full of tears. No love, No sympathy. I have nowhere to go! I knew that people like me do not have a career, would be fed in "jungle." Working smart now is necessary.

Our personnel manager is a blonde lady. In my observation, she is the key character to change my fate. She is successful and is married with children. I am jealous of her body. She is a strong woman. I warned myself "be polite, be gentle."

"Good Morning" my first conversation to her or say monologue. She glanced at me no answer. I am visible now! I encouraged myself to do it every morning, when I met her. Little by little, I find that sometime she skipped her breakfast. Another busy day she looked paled. "Good Morning Laura have you had breakfast today?" She is surprised by me but still no answer. "It is not polite to keep in silence when your employee is greeting you." She flashed and thanks to me. From then on our conversation is mutual. I studied customers and store input for years. Now I can give my opinions when we are greeting. Much information is original for her. She learnt to know. Yet she is still proud of her. I cannot tolerate this unbalance anymore. Let it snow.

This time the company has a crucial meeting about the new trend of products' choice. I invited her for supper before the meeting. Candle lights & red wine; sex in the hotel after my report. Tomorrow, with big breakfast, she succeeded in the meeting. Am I easy to forget? My sperm is wasted in vain in condom? After that meeting, the company offers the project manager. She appointed me. My career begins that day. Customers are my customers; I even has power to hire & fire my project's employee. ***Now*** I can say I have little man's syndrome.

17

My First Dose

May 27th 2014, I did my first putting down sleep operation. That is like a big dream! A nurse laid down an oxygen mask on my face. The smell was strange. Then an anaesthetist put the drug in my vein. Also they took off my eye glasses. My dreams began. First I felt I had almighty power. I recalled my history from China to Canada. How did I devote myself to my fatherland? I experienced fails and excited. Suddenly, I realized that this is a hospital. I was bounded in a cell like a Jell-O box. I saw some out space biological. I touched death. Struggling back, I saw doctor sort out medical bottles. The nurse help me get rid of bloody cloth and wiped me. I do not knew what exactly happened. I asked her, did I have period just now? She said, "No. You just finished operation. This blood is from it." I was still in bed; the drops all drilled in my body. I looked up; my blood pressure; GEE, 151-95 too high. The nurse said that, during the operation, once it was even as high as an alarm level. God really blessed me. I got up. The bed all blood; my hospital gowns were the same situation. It looked like I just gave birth! Oh my dreams, I cannot forget forever. In front of me, my husband besides me. I totally come back. I compared my fantasy and my new marriage. I am happy that he companies me here and took care of me. I will cherish our life experiences and go together for ever. Last but not least, the hospital gave us a taxi card, so we can take taxi for free to go home. Thank you Canada, thank you all!

My Second Dose

June 16th 2014 Monday, I got my second dose in Toronto Sun Rise Hospital. Surprise, surprise … I met the same doctor in emergency room. I went there at 12:40 pm. The operation began at 8: 40pm. The doctor is Chinese descent; his father from Hung Kong, his mother from Taiwan. He is OK, but nurse said that he is pretty sharp to nurses; yet treats patients well. First he saw me in operation room; he said that, "it will be very quick." I said, "I do not need too quick; cure is the most important." then an anaesthetist put me down to sleep. I was actually still awake and rather calm. I felt comfortable. Then I suffered severe pain. I was yelling and twisted. When a nurse bandaged my cut, I could not stop crying. Blood, high blood pressure waiting for going home. The nurse taught me how to shower and kept the wound clean, so I may not need to do the procedure again and again. This time they did not give us taxi fee. My husband payed it 15 dollars.

18

The Blue Fingernails

Failyer comes from a lower class family. Her father is tall and handsome; her mother has a good figure. On the surface, everything is fine. Yet her mother suffers from memory lost and heritage to her. The whole family relies on her father's income. When she went to school, Failyer had to go to some special class to study. Struggling at school makes her unpopular and low self-esteem. After community college, both her parents and she want to find a man to marry. Failyer is fair hair, grey eyes, good body size and tall. For her to find a simple job seems not a problem. Soon, she becomes a cashier in a local food market. The worries pop up. She cannot remember the prices of goods; also she is easy to forget what she should do. Customers have a longer waiting time. The boss did not fire her but put her on night shift.

Every day before go to work, she carefully combs her hair; and polishes her fingernails in blue colour. She longs for a cowboy; handsome and rich who can save her away from the life that she lives. Once she asked her father why he married her mom. He said: "I cannot forget she said I am handsome." How easy it is! And how big effort he contributes. A few male customers purposely leave phone numbers or ask future contact. But they are non-white. It is not what she expected. Afraid to tell the men her gene problem is a gap to marriage too. The blue fingernails unveil her deep beaten heart.

19

Improve Place

Today I went to Improve Place to pick up my check. I like here. Every time I see the familiar faces; I just feel going back home. I say hi to my worker. I like Robinson. She taught me some kitchen job. Brian and a lady worker can use computer well. I just learnt and practice.

Brian is quiet. He is a single. Working in Improve Place is an easy job for him. Most people have their ambitions, which may not be the real lives of them. He thinks that if he is a soldier; he sacrifices his love and life to save others. He also wants to lead a way which makes the clients- disabled individuals have a happy life. He believes in God's love and almighty. He tries his best to show our heavenly father's love. I often remember his thoughtful remind and teaching.

He had a shadow. Life can only donate once. If a soldier dead in the field, he cannot be back. Brian likes his work and maintains well. He wishes that he could create a miracle- a successful model of a client who will be a star both in the working place and family life. At this point he is prudent for every small step, because he does not want clients feeling hurts either. Sometimes I think about his life. Has he broke down with his girl friends? Had he thought that his life is happy or suffering? Single is a life style that he leave to him and also a hope to some of his clients. Heavenly Father' unmeasurable Love gathers us together.

We have many female clients. He saw their weakness and hope. He noticed me for a while. He got one of my essay. 2 years ago, I worked in Trivita Company. I showed him my income (pretty good at that time) and hoped his join. Yet he was not interest. Since then, he began to notice me. I also need his help to improve my English writing and more trainings in Improve Place. I thank him a lot.

20

To My Parents: 1

I was an immigrant to Canada for over 13 years. My mental illness has always disturbed me. I dropped out of school three times, and went into hospitals over 15 times. I got disability benefits from the government for years. My parents live in China, so they could not help me too much.

Missionaries met me just in front of my room. I told them what I suffered and I really did not know what I should do next at that time. They introduced to the Book of Mormon to me. Elder Pearson and elder Homer brought me to our church and bishop baptized me. At the beginning, I felt that in our church I could met a lot of members; most of them are very thoughtful and friendly. I also have some social support. Also the church has many activities such as dancing, BBQ, parties, or meetings. As an active member, I totally enjoy.

This year, I went to temple trip. I learned a lot of brand new knowledge. I like temple's clothes and people who service or endowment. God blesses me and I find my new better half. We live together and most of time we are happy.

I knew that I am the only member in our family. You did not want to seal with me in heaven that I believe in. I respect your choices. I love you- my parents. God bless you.

21

To My Parents 2.

Life is tough for me. I find that I lose interest in learning something. I seldom read the Bible and the Book of Mormon. I cannot share my testimony in front of people in the church. I joined the church over 10 years. I decided to change this situation. Now I Read the Book of Mormon every day. I try to learn some difficult words that make me understand the book more.

Parents are the first teachers for the children. God is the rightest teacher and leader for our whole life. When I just joined church, I am really felt that some members contribute their time and money to our church may not be worthy. Yet, 8 years passed, I love my church just like loving my family. In our church, we listen to our apostles, our bishops, and our peers. God is so near us and touchable. Reading is also a way to purify our minds. According to reading and pray, I correct my actions. The proper behaviours make me look good and feel good. Meanwhile, God helps somebody who helps himself. Only I want to improve myself; I can do it well. Otherwise, I am just like some poor seeds which cannot have plenty products.

My dear father and mother, I know that you do not believe in God. I just write down these letters for my personal testimony to proof that God is real. I believe that one day, we can share the message with each other.

22

To My Dear Parents 3

Time flies so fast. I miss you more often than ever. My favourite thing is chatting with you on-line. We can see each other face to face; we can chat as long as possible. Our church often gives us some DVDs about Jesus Christ, God or other key characters that makes me excited. I feel that I know God and listen to God's words. The most sensation part is that we do a lot of performance. We have church's parties to show them. I like Steak Centre's shows. They have a choir. Other church's programmes are fabulous too. For many talent people church's show is a good chance to practices.

When I see some brutal parts of the church' DVD, I tear. I am appreciated our heavenly father's love. His love is higher above than the highest mountains. He promised us the salvation. **Great is measure our father's love.** Every time I see Him and his only begotten Son with white clothes. I recalled Jesus Christ pours his precious blood for all of us. The lily white gown with Holy Spirit is our future lives too.

Here I think our daily pray. Pray to our heavenly father. Our earthly father gives us flesh and blood bodies; our heavenly Father gives us souls to choose what is wrong or right. When we are not sure what we should do, we pray. When we have difficulties or other persons have troubles we pray. Our Father will listen and will help us at any time.

I wish that my parents baptized at our church. We all reunion in our temples. That would be nice. I know the wonderful temples and temple clothes.

Note: *quoted by think about Him lyrics*

23

To My Dear Parents 4

Every time I heard the song "I am a child of God"; I feel sore. My childhood was miserable. My father was busy for his career; my mom seldom showed love to me. School boys bullied me. They were much older than me and not just one or two. I was confused by personal relationship. My biggest hobby was reading which really saved me for years. But I was sick when I was 17 years old. I still continued my education until I was 30 years old. Then I married. I worked to support two persons' family.

Before I joined the church, I did not know what the meaning of love is. I do not know that love means given, tolerate, and sacrifice. Nobody seems to sacrifice for me. I went to the church and learned the Bible and the Book of Mormon. I began to know that we also have a heavenly Father, who has a salvation plan which is beyond any career and achievement. Under His arms, I understand feelings of people. I embraced love from Him and the members.

For me the strangest part of the God's plan is after death. God judges us to each level. In China, we do not believe in God. We believe that people die and all is finished. Now Jesus Christ is a perfect model for all of us. If we keep God's commandment, one day, we will live with Him in heaven.

My earthly parents now are old and retired. I cannot take care of them since I am in Canada. My childhood's shadow is on and off. I learn to forgive, tolerate, and love. I never feel that I am so mankind. I left my hometown over 11 years. Endless missing tortures me. My relatives and my friends are my strangers. I love Canada more. Here, I get my new hope and began to know why I come to the earth. I grew up here and changed my major life goals here. God bless us; we love Him forever!

24

Queen of Mercy

In the sky, the stars are shining. One of our Arabian princesses follows Allah's words and becomes a new Queen. She was royal highness; she is a symbol of wisdom. Witness! She wrote her true love's name, so beautiful! She is the teacher of royal's princesses also a doer.

Our Great Common Wealth sidelong glanced her for a while. Royal Prince Harry began to learn Arabian and the Book of Qur'an. Thousands of days and nights, he learnt with his tutors by Allah's guide. "My Queen, how can I sit beside you now?" He wrote a letters to her. His heart is pumped. He knew that she is the best for him. The Queen got his letters. She read it and reply to one. In it, she for the first time wrote down her true love's name- Harry, so beautiful signature! Prince Harry received the letters. Her handwriting deeply moved him. Prince Harry studied harder to be perfect. One crescent moon, he felt it urgent to call her. She said that "I love you, royal blue blood." "I love you too, my Queen." said Prince Harry.

The whole world is upset down. Muslim experienced the hardest time since ever. All of these could not shake Prince Harry's belief. In his mind, she is supreme. One day, Prince Harry called her again with confidence. "Could you marry me?" *"I never ever love no one before you.* You are my only true love. I am pretty. I can fight" the Queen said. Soon they married. Since then Muslim men open their hearts to marry the Great Common Wealth girls and love them forever. After that they fight for Muslim to win.

Note: quotation from Pretty Boy lyrics.

25

Bob's Episodes

Bob (cat) is a big boy now. His mating season comes. The first outdoor experience is awful. He went out and immediately down to veranda. I rushed to catch him but he already disappeared. Then the massive searching job began. Our friend Mervyn my husband and I go door to door; back yard to back yard even crossed streets. I called him everywhere; I blamed myself; I was afraid that I could not see him again. First time I let my husband found a touch to look at veranda; nothing found. Second time the same, because there are too many staff. The third time I looked at veranda, I found Bob sat there. Mervyn went down street; we called him yet he could not respond. My husband finally brought him back. We tried many ways-using cat cookies, can food, scared him by knocking the wall. All failed. Finally, I said that I crawled in to rescue him. Mervyn and my husband began to pull the wood from the veranda. Then I laid down to come in. I am 270 pounds. The veranda is low and has a lot of raccoons' shits. The only thing I cared was my baby-Bob. After over 2 meters I found him. I pulled him back; he scratched me. I let my husband pushed a carrier to me. He used a long stick to push it near me. I hold Bob and put him in carrier. I kicked carrier to the exit; they got Bob. I slowly came out. My body stick lots of dirt. We went home then ordered Chinese food to celebrate. Mervyn pointed Bob to say: "from now on, you move to the bottom." At this time, I just find many bruises on my body, some even bleeding. My watch was scratched too. Bad bob.

Bob was put in the carrier on 9 pm. In the morning10 am, we used cart to drag him to vet. On the road, he is very quiet (Prince was very noise). The vet asked us some simple question then let us go home to wait. At 3 pm, we picked up him. The vet said that "everything is good." when he went back home, he still jumped here and there; looked like nothing happened. Our old friend Mervyn came and blamed him "Although did the operation, no difference."

26

Tom & Sexy Lin

Tom and Lin both work in St. Joseph Hospital Cleaning Department. Monday, they clean the top floor- the seventh floor.

Tom is a blonde, gold hair, blue eyes, 41 years old, Russian guy. Lin is a Chinese lady. They work like a golden couple. Tom is like a brother to show the jobs and leads Lin. Lin's skin is white and shining but has some sun burn. The most amazing part is that she has two pairs of gold earrings. She leans to Tom in mind and job duties. "You do something; I do less; because I am a lady!" She thought. She did so. Tom likes fantasy. Tom felt that he has whole bunch of followers. Yet from work, he did most. He and she shows a racial equality. They work on it and make it happen. Lin likes Tom to call her June, since she was born in June. Lin always gets to relax, so she also gives back to Tom. At lunch, Tom can taste many kinds of Chinese food. His favourite food is Chinese dumplings. That is his dream.

On a long winter day they got together go out for dinner. "A +A" they are used to it. Not too much words, they took adventure. Two culture melted together. Golden boy conquered the Eastern girl's heart and body. Shaking bodies and boobies; love is so easy and so long time waiting.

Tomorrow, it is a shining day too. They work harder and closer more often. The blonde boy or say man said that if the hospital fired one of them, he would go. But most people like him more.

Under the blue light, Lin or say June wishes that they had gone together forever.

27

My University

Poor I studied at College of Toronto. My dream was to be a doctor. After two years of hard working, I decided to be a psychiatrist, because it is easier than other operation doctors.

My score is always in middle. How can I survive in this nightmare? I went to church to ask God. I got down on my knees to pray and pray. "What kind of songs?" The church thyme team is singing. I saw them. Most of them turn to their knees to centre, right hands hold the thyme books. I knew what I shall do now. From then on, every time I ask questions on my teachers. My left hand holds a book and I turn my knees toward them and my whole body leans toward the teachers.

"Am I so stupid?" "Am I not a top class student?" my heart knelled down too. I knew how good I am. Most teachers did accept me and help me more than other proud students. But female students did not like me. In their eyes, I am a toad.

One of my professors is a gay. He noticed this. One day, he said to me: "Your essay needs to be improved; tomorrow afternoon 1 pm you go to my office." Innocent I followed his order. "Come in please!" I walked in and closed the door for a good manner. He sat in the chair and said, "Take off your trousers and underwear, please." My butts even became red, but I did follow. He is clear and wise. His biggest hobby is English Discipline. I held on a chair's back. This time I stand straight. Every time he caned me, I need to answer his questions. I felt his anatomy knowledge is brilliant. He knew my brain and body very well. I did not know that it is a leap for my knowledge or a body abuse. At least, I got what

I want. I count every cane; totally 99. I wish he could give himself a dime score. Now I am Allah.

Until now, I still clearly remember this lesson. Thanks to my professor. I am a gay now. My girls all refused me. The girls want me, who are not psychiatrist at all. Poor me.

28

Police Stations

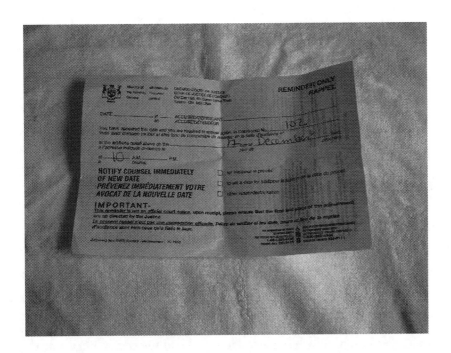

April 1st, 2015 I was discharged from Toronto Cardtons Hospital's psychiatric ward. My husband came there to pick me up. Yet when we just walked to the elevator, two policemen stopped me. Then they handcuffed me and let my husband's go to 52 Police Division. I was in the police car there too.

In the Police Station, they asked me many questions. They told me that my psychiatrists charged me, so they arrested me. They forced me to take off my shoes and went to a discipline room. That room is as big as 3/5 of an Olympic swimming pool, Marble floor, Marble bench. I was just by myself. I did not wear socks; it was icy cold. I heard outside policemen say that I am brave. I did not care. There is a toilet in the room, so I was not worried about thirst. After a while, I felt cold; I knocked at the steel door. A black policewoman opened the window on the door and said that I should wait for the police from upstairs. I continued to wait, I could not sit on the bench, since it was too cold; maybe I was too weak, in the hospitals for two months. Finally I lost my patience. I began to kick the door with my bare feet, because my hands were too painful to knock on the door any more. Outside somebody talked. I did not care. I kicked the door no matter what. Almost half an hour, one police kicked the door loud from the other side. I felt upset and kicked hard too. Then I calmed down. They had police boots but I was bare in feet. I stood on the marble floor, and thought how long should I wait? Soon a policeman opened the door, held my jacket and threw my eye glasses on the floor. He pushed me to walk fast and twisted me. At last, he opened a cell door; one hand pushed me directly on the steel toilet. My feet were in the air too. In the meantime, I felt Allah's hand protect my poor heart. I survived. Facing God, he is sin. I still had bare feet and sat there. It was a little bit warmer than that room. Some prisoners were in the different rooms. Some were crying; some were pleading. I was quiet. I was still confused about why I was here instead of going home to rest. I did not know how long I should wait. That policeman came here again and said: "You behave yourself, after which, I will do your finger prints." I felt that I almost died here. No freedom, no mercy, no one listened to my voice! He came back, let me wear my shoes and pushed me again to a room to do the finger prints and take pictures. I saw the policeman, holy cow! He is over 2 metre's height. His name tag is "W. Smith." Who knows? Sometime, they use pseudo name. He is much stronger than me; even a man may could not fight against him. Here it is a police station. If I just do self-defence, they may kill me for no reasons. I gave up totally. He did my finger prints very carefully. No missing spot. I felt that it is an insult! Then, he walked me back to the cell. They left me an out of date cheese sandwich and a box of juice for me. I have diabetes, I should not drink juice; yet I was already starving and thirsty. I finished them. After a while, they transferred me to 55 Division, which is a jail for women. Before I went to the court truck, I saw that policeman's arm's tattoo "勇" a Chinese character, which means brave and good at fight.

It is hard to imagine that if he was furious at home. He would pushed his wife to the toilet or not. He did not respect woman. "Brave" in bed, or sex abuse. Maybe, I thought too much. His behaviour really separated me with police; which really made me think that police are violent.

The 55 Division's truck came. They handcuffed two of us to the truck. This time they gave me my eye glasses. There are no handles for climbing the truck. I could not go to the truck by myself. One policeman helped me. It is a long drive. I could not tolerate it. My nose was bleeding. In 55 Division, first the sergeant asked me some questions. Then, they checked my clothes and body again and let me go to my cell. It is number 8. In the book of Qur'an, number 8 means dog. In the cell. There is an iron bed, no pillow or blanket. A steel toilet with water fountain, better than the discipline room. About 5 o'clock pm, I got a cheese sandwich and a box of juice. There are at least 4 persons in the jail. Some were crying, some knocked on the bars. I did not have the night time medication so I did not sleep. Once, I pooed; the police who had monitor, reminded me faster. Once I lay down in the iron bed, because it was cold and I was so weak I could not stop coughing. The police showed the unpleasant. About 12 am, they gave me another cheese sandwich and a box of wild berry juice. I consumed them. And I used the juice box to drink water. Sometimes, I was really crazy, I wanted to random shooting in my heart, yet I even could not bare hands to do so. At 6 am, they handcuffed us again and sent us to court at college park.

A man interviewed me and gave me a duty consul. I went to the court, and got bail. Now, I still did not think that I am guilty. Let the judge have the final say. My bishop even wanted to leash me with his belt, because of this. I did not know that who tell him this. I knew that I am innocent! God bless me.

29

Improve Place 2

Confucius said: "Friend from far away, joyful?" May 11th, 2015 Toronto Improve Place welcomes our friends from 4 different Improve Places. One from Australia, one from Pennsylvania USA, one from Prince Edward Island, one from Ontario.

In the morning, my husband and I woke up earlier and took the TTC to our Improve Place. When we got there, it was just 7 am. Our club house opens at 8:30 am. We found a coffee shop and waited there. The weather was a little bit chilly, but we were excited. My husband wore a suit; I wore a skirt. Our club house even offers a free breakfast! Finally, the door opened. We came in and said hello to our fellows. At 9 am, our club house president had a speech to introduce our guests. I like them. They are the successful members of Improve Places. Breakfast was buffet. I was very nervous about meeting new friends. I found it difficult to talk to them because I was worried that they may not like me. I am a big person, however I did not want to give them the impression that I am a heavy eater, so my husband and I only ate a little bit. After breakfast, the members went to different floors to practice and study. Many members where were talkative, busy and welcome.

At noon, we went to the basement cafe shop to have lunch, which cost 2 dollars. I did not like the lunch. I just bought a bowl of soup. I sat at the table with the other members. This time we broke the ice and had some conversation. I met a lady from PA; she has three kids and works full time. Compared with her, I really need to improve myself. Since I am a housewife and no children. I find David from PEI handsome. I do have some friends from PEI, they are very nice people. I met a lady who is originally from Toronto, but now lives in Australia with her husband who is Australian. She married an Australia man and went there for live. She wears a big diamond ring. Last but not least, a man with two crutches from our province. I like his spirit, by the way that day was his birthday. Improve Place made a birthday cake for him. He was very happy.

May 15th, 2015 our club house did a BBQ. We enjoyed the BBQ together. We said greetings; we discussed many topics. One guest was interested in homosexuality. Our club house locates in the central of homosexuality shelters.

Time pass quickly, by May 22nd, 2015 our guests said good-bye to our Improve Place members. Some of our members felt hurt to see them go. I stayed at home because my husband did not feel well. I bless them: "Have a good trip."

Thanks to all Improve Places. We make friends here; we grew up here; we can say no to loneliness and marginalization. We have opportunities to study, exercise and entertainment here. Thanks to our staff and members.

30

Church and Wellesley Food Stand

Today, June 6th, 2015 I went to Improve Place for fun. I came too early, so I went to 519 Church Street to rest. People there were quiet, not busy at all. I even made a friend and communicated each other. 11am, I went to Improve Place. My old buddies also came. We joked around and exchanged new ideas. Lunch here, I did not like. I went to Church and Wellesley food stand.

This food stand is just besides TD bank. I am a regular customer. There is a man there to serve me at this time. I ordered Polish sausage, well done; 4 dollars. He whistled and did it. A father with his son passed by and ordered 2 hot dogs. The son is very cute who jumped on the homosexual flag on the ground. My order was done. I also chose Oliver, onion, pepper, relish, and corn to eat. I went to Rexall Drug Store to eat and window shopping. It is really delicious. When I finished it, I tried to go back to Improve Place, but I could not. My legs were weak, I even could not walk. I did not eat buffet. It was not that much full for a sausage dog. The 94 A bus was coming. I got on bus heading home. The weather was perfect. I loved it, yet I could not see the scenery so clear. I felt that I was drunk. The only thing I wanted to do was sleep. I even wanted to fire my psychiatrist. Then I changed from the bus to the subway, I was still unclear. The worst part was to take bus 71 A to home. I slept besides the driver.

Going home, I paralysed in the chair and headache. I told my husband that I preferred to go to hospital, however he was not interested. He wished that we would rather stay at home. I slept until 3' a clock pm. I ate the sausage at 12 pm.

I must document that for everybody, in case the people just like the father and the son still go there to eat and damage their brains. I did not understand where the police are? Where do they eat their food? They have guns and orders. Please stand out and do something to stop this dirty business.

31

The Little Man in General- Merchandise 2

Last time, he was promoted to project manager, yet he failed and became a cashier. He had already fulfilled this underdog business. The big ambition came out. Small men often are smarter. Many of them study to be an electrician. He also wished to do it. As the saying goes: "A great teacher produces a brilliant student." Finding a brilliant teacher he racked his brain. Finally he chose Mr. Brian to be his teacher.

Brian is a father of two. His family is a middle income family. This time the little man was not shy, because he thought he can do it. Brian is 1.80 meters height. He also thinks that he should give this little man a chance. A strict teacher produces outstanding students. Brian did have some students. The first week, Brian let him read an electrical professional book and let the small man follow him here and there. The small man felt interested. Then he began to asked questions, and thinking about the theories that the book was written by. Brian was happy too. Once the little man offered to fix the problem and succeeded. Brian has a woman student; she is 5.10 feet height. She is smart too. Yet Brian never let them compete each other. Since the little man has some improvement; he tried to replace the teacher. He actively answered the others questions and showed his new technique. One day the teacher thought that it is a good time to show the little man's truth. He got a ladder and let the small man to change the light on the roof of General - Merchandise's McDonald. The customers were eating now. The ladder could not touch the customers. The little man climbed on the ladder and tried to reach the light which had problem. However he really could not. The customers were very co-operative. They stood up and moved the chair. The little man reset the ladder but when he climbed on the top, he still could not reach the light. How embarrassed it is. This time Brian called the woman student to change the light. She did it without effect. The little man had even more low self-esteem. Yet he did not want to quit. He knew that this is the best teacher he could find. The practise time finished. General – Mechanise made a decision that the woman was hired.

Where is the little man? He disappeared in the concrete jungle.

32

Prince and Cinderella Review

The splendid royal ball made the Prince Charming fall in love with Cinderella. Her natural virtues conquered the audiences' hearts. Facing royal power, rich, nobility, and motherhood, she was magically changed almost everything.

Compared with other women, I seldom noticed my dresses, hair styles and my makeup, which lead to my husband say that: "My only book is women's look." I guess that I must be Cinderella's half-sisters in his eye!

I do not often see the life performance. Watching TV is much different from life performance. In the movie version, they changed actors and actresses very often. But in drama, they almost did not change anyone. Everybody needs playing a lot. This Cinderella version is the University of Toronto one. My favourite part is the one mouse and one rat. They are just like me big boom or belly, humor and charming and knew how to communicate with audiences. I love these two people's acting skills. Another big surprise is that at the very beginning, one male actor played Cinderella's half-sister who made me recalled one sex worker in our neighbourhood. He is gorgeous. He even made me recalled one Chinese actor when I was 14 years old. I could not be separated from them for a while.

When the show finished and the police car passed me, I just felt that I am in Canada and I am a woman. It is very coincidentally, when I took subway, that sex worker dressed up and made up well in front of me. I thought that he is the actor. I walked to talk to him. Yet I found that he is not. Arts sometimes are purified but brutal. I still wish that it is he play in today's stage.

Let's talk something about Cinderella. She has a beautiful face. The Prince Charming complained that there are many ugly faces that he could not stand. Cinderella lived with her step-mother and two half-sisters. They forced her to do all the housework. She heard this chance (royal ball) which may changes her life. She longed to be a princess too. Finally, her family went to the royal ball and she too went to the royal ball with a fair lady's help. Crystal shoe is the classic plot. They also adopted it, however they deleted plan B- step-mother married the King and the King finally let her go back to her home. Here it is a happy ending that everybody moved to the palace.

The Prince Charming is a royal hero. He saved Cinderella in the fire and the water. He is every lady's idol. In the real society, we do meet many opposite ones. My ex-husband is one of them. He did not earn money; he did not care about me at all. When I was in the hospital he spent all the money. Of course, I divorced him. I do not want to be a royal princess, yet if somebody is like the Prince Charming who can take care of me, I will take care of him for life! Even we can seal in heaven! That is why Cinderella is rare.

33

Joel Smith and Me

Improve Place gave me a tutor whose name is Joel Smith. First day we were together, which was genuine sensation. I seldom know that my essays really need to be revised, except for grammar. He is the first teacher who pointed out my strong and weak parts. I understand English better. When I went home, I recited his corrections to improve my writing. Our second meeting, I just wrote two essays; I passed to him. He said that he will revise them for next time. Then we did not meet for a long time.

He maintains a good shape while he also studies at school to be a teacher. 11 years ago I studied education too. His belly is flat and has some drainage tubes in it. It may lead him to get some infection and severe pain. In his mind a teacher's handsome is beyond his knowledge. He may pursuit a beautiful and rich gentile lady. I have a big tummy. I cannot say I am beautiful; yet my husband always compliments me. I am satisfied. Casual life makes me lazy. When I see our fellows improving themselves day by day, I felt that I am almost nothing. Life may play a joke on you every minute. My tutor has this big ambition to teach outside Canada under this physical condition. He is a hero! Some of our members do not want to do anything to make our clubhouse shine.

I lack of exercises especially after marriage. Before I married my husband George, I had a romantic life. I had lovers, boyfriends and acquaintances. Yet I did not transfer diseases. Some men did love me; some did not. I did not contact them often, just for emergencies. Once I even went to fitness club to do excises every day, then I met my husband in Improve place.

My number 1 concern is Islam. I support them no matter how. Politics is my first life, nothing else. My writing is my Shakespeare. That is why I wish I could have a teacher to lead me, guide me, and discipline me. I go to church on Sundays. There I can purified myself and keep going. I read the Book of Mormon and others which inspire me to be better. I think that this is the reason why Improve place found Mr. Joel to be my tutor.

Love on first sight, If not, no respect at all. I cannot do the tummy tuck; I do not want to be an artificial one. Recently I see Joel in Computer Class. Nice catch. Young and energetic make him feel good and have confidence. He is one of our clubhouse's future generation. God bless him.

34

Man's Tear

Bill started to learn to play baseball when he was 5 years old. He just loved it. Every morning his father sent him to the playground in a different city, which is the nearest one he can go. As a father for 7, he did sacrifice a lot. Bill is a fair hair blue eyed white kid. He looks exactly like his father.

Bill could both pitch and hit well. He is a smart one. Time flies. Now he is a high school student. Of course he still plays baseball. He wish that he could be a professional player. His mother is the principal of his high school, which really makes him proud of it. Training is the hardest part. The coach never let him have a breath! He pitches, runs the bases and bats. After training, he felt his legs extreme traumatically. Also he really met many excellent players- severe competition. Sometimes, he thinks that he is a little merman, even cannot walk! Besides baseball, he is a teenager Billy now. Many girls likes him. He did not want to waste time for it. A girl who is special whose name is Billie. Bill had different feeling for her. They study in the same class and in the spare time, she watches his games. His team seldom loses. He is the marrow of the team! He notices her cheers. He likes her too, but secretly.

Once, the team lost the final game, because he did not catch the ball. The coach is immediately upset and said that I won't give you another chance! Billy was a loser? He questioned himself. Billie was in front of him. No word, no plead. She admires his perfect body for life, 6 feet 2 inch height like his mother (6 feet). She even did not know how to touch him. She did a hand job for him. And then they went back their own homes. As a principal and mom, she did not say some words to console her favourite's son. He should grow up now!

Then the daily routine comes back now. Training and training, he motivates himself to do it better. The coach did not like him anymore. The new series began. He became a bench player! His whole life is a dream just like a bubble. He tried his best to exercise better to change his coach's mind. He thinks that this is his last chance. The final comes again in his team! He sits on the bench to watch the game. Score is a 3:3 tie. He suddenly stood up. The coach looked at him and called for a change. He is on the field now! He plays first base and he did not give him any excuses to lose again. Nice catch! Again! Perfect catch! His team won. He became his team's hero again! He saw Billie. Yes she is there, but he did not come to her.

Many year past, when they met again. He was a just a common man. He has broken his thumb and could not pursue his professional career anymore. She is still here, but he said: "Pass let it pass." Tears for both.

35

Man of the Sun

Leo is a tall, strong and white guy. In his mind, most of women like him, although he is just a construction worker. His girlfriend is a beautiful one who drives him crazy. At night, they feel so wonderful. Leo really is a lion in bed! In the daytime, he still has energy to finish his job. Life seems fantastic.

Construction workers can earn decent money. How to spend the money Leo and his girlfriend had a big ambiguity. Every time Leo wants to buy a house, yet his girlfriend said that, "I want to travel." He follows her idea. They did have a prince and princess' life. Now he began to think of marriage. The best way to show the commitment to marriage is the wedding ring. He drove her to the jewelry store. She was surprised! Yet she said that "I do not deserve it. We are good friends." Leo is sad and confused. How come she does not deserve it? Why does she not want to get married? One day, he followed her. He found that she was with a man in a bar, then together to go. Now he knew why she refused to marry. He recalled many years he spent his savings to please her. She just fool him. No way, I won't let you go so easy. He called her. She came and acted just like nothing had happened. Leo asked her why she went out with other men. She is blushed. She said that, "I love your sex and money but not yourself." He collapsed and let her go.

The following day, he did not go to work. He was sick at home for over one week. He could not trust women anymore. He went back to work. Lack confidence and energy made him clumsy. As a lesson, he shaved his head. In the middle of summer, wearing a safety helmet, he felt cool.

Since Toronto has a big gay society, Leo hung up with gays now. Man and man are best friends; just like people said that dogs are man's best friends. He relied on it. He is addictive to it so as to affect his job! Now his co-workers all laugh at him. We need a Great Lishen, not a disabled one. When he heard of this, he knew that he is wrong. He grew back his hair and worked hard at his job now. The scatter sunshine makes him happy.

36

James Twins

In the Church of Jesus Christ of Latter Day Saints. Toronto Ward, Brother James has twin boys. When I first time saw them, they were about one year old. I never can separate them. Their mother takes care of them a lot. When they are much .older, I still remembered that one of them held mom's leg; the other was jealous of him and pushed him away then held mom's leg. They are so cute. Once both of them were crying at the sacrifice meeting, Mrs. James one hand pulled one boy; the other hand pulled the other one out of the room. I did not think that I had that much strength. At that time, they were toddlers.

Time flies fast. They are about 12 years old now. They already serve sacrifice meeting and did well. Both of them look much like their father. They are quite just like their parents in public. They enjoyed church's culture both at home and in the church. Once I saw one of them that there is a red spot on the side of the nose. I knew how to separate them now. They are kind and shy and truly the children of God.

Every Mondays, it is our church's family day. At this day, family members need to get together for all kinds of purposes. Our former bishop James and his family must very creative. I saw his second daughter's drawings. Hopefully, one day they will share their success stories for us.

37

Control Our Young

Toronto Pride Parade opened our minds and stimulated our unlimited imagination. Facing so many temptations, a woman with her top off took a picture with Liberal Party leader Justin Trudeau. In Vancouver Pride, a teenage girl did almost the same thing; just covered her nipples. Many people may think that these incidents are unacceptable. Yet from the other side, as a Canadian political royal – the eldest son of former Canadian Prime Minister Pierre Trudeau did not refused them to thousands of miles away; on the contrary, he did shoot a photo with Toronto girl. He let her sweet dream become true. If it changed to other parties' leaders for this situation, they refused to do so; may even embarrassed these girls. They will have a permanent mark in their young minds. Justin Trudeau's enthusiasm is positive.

Let us talk about the Vancouver girl. As an unmarried teenage girl, she is still her father's. Over exposed she is improper. From this event I think that she will learn something for the future. So we should not too much hype to it. Justin Trudeau was a teacher. As a teacher, he gave love more than punishment.

Justin Trudeau as the youngest party leader of the four parties did not support the Gulf War. Let us see what Harper did. Sometimes he just as busy as a beaver follows with USA's footstep. For example: he supported USA president to control Iran's nuclear weapon. (We still do not know whether they really have nuclear weapon or not.) They forced Iran signed the unfair treaty for 10 years! At this point, I support Trudeau's policy. "Liberal Party knows that Canada has an important role to play around the world in promoting peace and security." He said. (Quotation 24 Hours September 18th, 2015)

As a leader with natural leadership, he can accomplish his ambition. Canadian needs a new look both in nation and in the whole world. His father taught him and left Trudeau Time for Canadian history. He is a vivid witness. Let us welcome the second Trudeau Time!

38

A friend in deed is a friend in need

Now it is not a safe time for the whole world, especially Arabs. In TV news, we saw them to go to Europe or other places. The richest 5 Arab countries should unite the other countries which are true friends of them to fight for real equality and peace.

Now it is Canadian election. Liberal Party does not support sending troops overseas. If the Conservative Party wins this election, some Arabian countries will be under Canadian army's control. At this turning point, everybody should think what you should do? Sometimes a sum of money for the right side is very necessary.

Let us recall how much money the USA had got from the UAE, in the latest 10 years. We won't mention that Iran lost how much money and dignity since March 2015. Do Arab countries really want be occupied by other countries? It is time to change; it is time to show your generosity. You want violence or winter coats? You want a beautiful homeland or to be refugees?

Let's pray for united Arabs and show time.

39

Mervyn Johnston's Legend

His family: Mervyn was named after his mother's first boyfriend. The meanings are superman or frugal person. His grandpa from his father side was a police constable who was a chauffeur of Toronto chief police. He was a brave and smart one. His father was the only child of his grandpa and he was also a policeman. He worked at 11 Division, 52 Division and Old City Hall Court. Mervyn's uncle was a York Township chief of police then Metropolitan Toronto Deputy Chief and Chief of the Harbour Police.

Mervyn's mother was brilliant. She finished high school when she was 14 years old. Then she went to work as a civil servant because she needed to support her family. She married Mervyn's father and had 3 children, two boys and one girl. Her relatives are smart too. They all millionaires and had good jobs.

The worst thing that happened to this family was Mervyn's father died in brain cancer when he was just 42 years old. His mother did not get her husband's full pension as he died 10 days before qualifying. After his father died, his grandpa did take care of them a lot. Every Christmas he brought a lot of food to their house, especially chocolate. If at the end, nobody finished it, he would eat it all. Another huge loss was that Mervyn's younger sister she is a blonde; had mental illness when she was 18 years old. Many times she held a knife and cut down telephone wire; chased her mother. Once she knocked down 5 policemen by herself. Finally 6 policemen and a doctor caught her and sent her to hospital. Because of this, the antique furniture in their house was broken. She beat Mervyn several times. Once she used a butter dish to hit Mervyn's eyes. His both eyes became black.

She sometimes tried to commit suicide. She used electric hedge clippers to cut her neck. Mervyn tried to stop her yet she still left a scar on her neck. He loves his sister. He took care of her just like a father. She had some bad habits. She smoked in the house and addictive food. She died when she was 42 years old. Until now, Mervyn's brother still said that we are lucky; we survived after our 42 years birthday. Mervyn's brother is a brilliant one. Mervyn always said that he inherited their mother's genius. He finished his high school when he was 17 years old and finished university when he was 19 years old. He studied at University of Toronto just like Mervyn. He had 4 daughters. One died at 4 years old. His daughters are well educated. He is a multimillionaire too. He is a real estate broker. His 2 daughters married. The youngest one just graduated from Humber College. Mervyn gave 50,000 to each of his brothers daughters. He is a rich uncle.

His school year and career: Mervyn is a diligent and clever one. When he was 5 years old, he already read all the children's book in the library near his home. A bad boy his name was Robbie Pyle who broke Mervyn's right arm when Mervyn was 5 years old. So he just can use his left hand to write and did some work. Mervyn studied at University of Toronto. He graduated 6 times. Horner Bachelor Degree of Arts; Horner Bachelor Degree of Education; Master Degree in History, Master Degree of Library Science … One of his teacher cherished him and recommended him to Oxford University to study major in English. Yet he said that he needs to take care his mom and sister, he could not go. After graduated from University of Toronto, he did not find a professional job, part because the Library Science dean did not give him his degree in time. When he got it, he already graduated 6 months later. He was mad at the dean. Finally, he decided to be an accountant and stockbroker. He went to Humber College to study. He graduated 6 times there and got whole bunch of certificates.

In Mervyn's history, his first job is delivering newspaper. When he was young, he rode a bicycle to deliver newspaper. Since my husband is his classmate and best friend, he often help him to do so. Mervyn did all kinds of jobs. Once he unload the ship over 12 hours. That day he kept all his saving to his jacket pocket and put on the ship. After finished loading the ship, the ship left and then he found that his jacket was still in the ship. He was very sad and had no money to go home. He went to a gambling place. Somebody was pitiful him and gave him a little bit money and he used it won some money to go home. He also work in Nestle Chocolate Factory with my husband. But he just worked in part time.

His real career began after he finished the Humber College. He help people do the tax and he is also a stockbroker. He never loses. He is great! People trust his skill and personalities. Now he is very successful. He is a multimillionaire. Everybody wants to be his client.

His friends and social life: when Mervyn was in kind garden, everybody called him Merv. He lives one block away from our home; just 5 minutes' walk. Every Wednesday he goes to our home to help my husband with his financial stuff. Sometimes we treat him some food. We are best friends. He is my mentor too. He often helps me revise my essays. I learnt a lot from him both in academic and personalities. Merv is still single. He loved a girl and made love with her when he was 21. I guess that he must do not want to catch 22. Merv did have many friends, most of them are disabilities. He is 66 years old and some of his friends already 70. For example: he had a friend in Western Ontario. He uses wheelchair. Once he went to Merv's house at 1 am. He drove the wheelchair very unstable, just like an orangutan flying here and there. Merv is afraid that he will fall in his property and Merv needs to pay his insurance. So Mervs never invited him to his home again. But they often go to restaurant to eat, and Merv treats him. He also contributes a lot of things to the Queen Elizabeth II, alrough he is poor. Merv always took care of his friends and made jokes for them. He has a hippy friends, who has 4 cats and they are university classmates. Louie is an alcoholic. Merv just can persuade him drinking less. Merv is jeopardy smart. When his mother was still alive, he and she watched jeopardy. Merv could answer all the questions and all correct. His mother even was amazed it. When Merv was young, he went to subway station and found newspaper in the garbage can to read it. Finally, the janitor gave him a key to open the garbage can. Merv still rides bike out. I am very worried about him. Our family and his clients rely on him. Mervyn is a superman. He did everything in his house. He cuts lawn; does garden; paints porch … Also he is super cheap. He just eats one potato at one time, he just buy the toast chicken in half price. His mower is 20 years old. But he like exercises. He constantly controls his weight. I cannot do it at all. Mervyn is a member of NDP. He often did volunteer work for them.

All in all I never met a person like Mervyn. He is a role model in my whole life. Every time I suggest that he should discipline me; he have never done so. He encourage me and teacher me in a different way. We like him.

40

One Day Supports Gay Society

The Liberal Party High Park-Parkdale rider Arif Virani has a big button with pride rainbow colors on it. It also has pride's Logo "Happy Pride, Liberal" and his full name. One day I wore it in public.

I wear a pure black dress with a button on it. It is beautiful and highly visible. Many people watch me like an alien. My left hand has wedding ring on it. (I am not gay.) But who knows? Some people treat me very offensively. For instance, some pull down the pants; some show the tattoos; some swear; some laugh at me; and some pop up from nowhere. I walk up Bay Street towards Dundas Square. Then I am heading to Church Street. Most Torontonians know that Church Street is Homosexuality Street. When I just came here, I felt safe and relaxed. Yet I suddenly felt the opposite way- much allure, temptations, criminals, and drug issues. Somebody say Hi to me or try to be acquaintances. I am not beautiful, just normal. This is my first time I feel popular.

I went back and went to Old City Hall. I have some issues there. The policeman saw me and said "wonderful." (I look up dictionary wonderful sometimes means fuck off.) Time is plenty. I began to tour Old City Hall. Here nobody notices me. I feel much better. After a while, I need to go to washroom. I could not find woman's washroom on the first floor, because it is locked. It is too late to go to other floors. Also I am embarrassed to ask people where is woman's washroom. I am afraid that they will ask me. Are you a man or woman? No problem, I rush into man's washroom. I went to a water closet. Dam! Somebody did not flush the toilet. This is not the first time I experienced it. I flushed it and peed. The closet is too small. I am 270 pounds. I made a lot of noises. I came out. The cleaner who is a man came in to put the toilet paper on. My face was immediately red. He was not too surprised.

After tour, I took the subway home. A man who carries "Better life fitness" sports bag walked besides me. He is masculine. I guess that he suggest that I should do exercises. On the subway, I felt I like an animal, not a human being. I just understand that the gay society needs acceptance as there is much pressure from everywhere, even from their own. For me just one day, I support them in public; now I know why people think they live on the edge. Toronto is a famous gay society in the whole world. Hopefully they were safer, happier and have a good home.

41

Tony Sant

Tony was our Improve Place's artist. He was popular for drawing feline family. Of course, he also drew others; for example: human beings, eagles and owls ... We loved him so much, yet he died in January 2014. Until now, my family has his 5 pictures- 3 cats and me and my husband portrait.

He loved drawing. Most of time we saw him in Improve Place; he grabbed a pen or pencil or whatever to draw. He drew portraits of anyone he saw. Some were very funny. I never heard that Tony had teachers. He longed for one but he did not get one. He drew my 18 years old cat "Harry," a tabby cat with green eyes. He said, "Oh that is a beautiful cat." In his drawing, Harry was quiet and focus. The long and bold nose I like very much. He also drew its shoulder. Then I showed my cat Prince's photo. At first he did not want to draw it, because he said that "it is too black!" Prince is a pure black cat. I begged him and gave him a dozen pencils. He drew my Prince. I like the eyes that he drew. It is vivid and looked at far away. He also used a lot of ink to draw its pure black fur. The small triangle nose was cute. Its whiskers have one side longer, one side shorter, since its head was facing toward the right side. For my youngest kitten "Bob" he drew a whole body. I like it too.

Tony also portrait of me and my husband. My husband's face is serious and pondering. I love his nose. Tony did drew it well- a big straight nose. That day my husband wore a jacket and shirt. Tony drew it too. The lips which he drew, I did not like it. My husband always smiles but he drew an angry lips. Overall I think that the portrait is good. Last but not least, it is my portrait. I wear glasses. He did a good job to draw the glasses. I like it so much. My nose is small and my mouth too. My hair just over my shoulders. He drew my hair with some natural curves. He said that my chin is big but he drew a little bit intentionally- shorter. That day I wear a pull over. He drew it well.

He also have many portraits in our clubhouse. But I could not take photos. One I like most is many many owls. On the top of his picture is a sun beam which is like the sun at noon. Then all the owls surrounded it, from far to near; small to big. In his life end, he got serious liver disease and often went to hospital. He drew the owls to mean wisdom, but in African culture, it also means a person is dying. In Arab, owls mean wizard and evil. I felt that Tony was afraid of death at that time, but I did not know whether I was right or wrong.

He is our clubhouse first artist who died. We have a corner for his arts. There are sketches, paintings, water colors, and so on. I wish that he was seen it in heaven.

42

Bill Clinton a Hero in My Mind

Bill Clinton was born in the first year of baby boomers. He was born in 1946, the same age as my father. I have admired him since I was in high school China. My father is a dean in university. He is a good influence for me too. In my spare time, I listened to the radio and watched TV. Bill Clinton's voice and perfect figure impressed me forever.

Teenager's crazy dream shuttered for decades. Now I am in Canada; I joined Liberal Party. I watch news almost every day. Bill Clinton is still active in his field. Sometimes I am online surfing. Compared with other presidents, he did accomplish much in US economics during his terms. His another policy is love or says sex- including homosexuality. He believes that love and sex can cure the pain. For himself, he is a sex manic. His life mainly is beauties and politics. He is a public successful icon. His policies are part of US reality.

Bill Clinton is also a very good father. He and his only wife have one daughter, just like my family. Yet, who would forget "Chelsea's Breakfast." US President-father made Harvard delivered admission to Chelsea, but she chose Stanford University. She helped her parents run for US President. Then she went to Oxford University to study PHD. Unlike her father, she pursued degrees one by one and become best. Bill was incomplete many times. In his time, might not have so many people cared about it.

43

TTC Driver is My Father

When I was young, I saw my father went to work with TTC uniform, which made me very proud. In my dream, I also want to be one of them. One day, my father came home, I pulled daddies' uniform and said that: "Dad, when I grow up, I also want to be a TTC driver!" My father saw me and sighed. "Son, you will be more successful!" I surprised. I knew that many of my classmates' parents were lawyers or practitioners. But what is the difference? I doubted.

One day, our teacher let us write an essay and draw a picture "what did you want to be in future?" I wrote that I wanted to be a TTC driver, just like my father with painting on. The teacher read the essay in the class. From that day, some of my classmates began to bully me severely. I was so isolated and shy. I did not tell anyone. My school marks dropped. I showed it to my father. He did not asked me why and then beat me hard. Now I knew what he wanted. I tried my best to catch up with others. Yet who cares you? - A TTC driver's boy? The teacher never favored me and was sarcastic to me a lot. I became unbalanced. Finally, I got mental illness. The bigger disaster began. The doctor gave me a wrong medicine and my illness became worse and worse. I have a total disability now.

Since then, I got limited ODSP money, and am idle. Sometimes, I went to the TTC; I saw the driver; I recalled my youthful dream and my reality. I hate my father. For me the only revenge way for TTC is avoiding the car fare. I did it for a couple of years. I felt happy and satisfied.

One day, I did my trick again. A TTC driver caught me and called police. Police came and found that I have mental illness and my father is a TTC driver.

They let me call my father. I beg them let me go. I promised that I would never do it again. Police called my father. I was scared to die. Soon my father came. When he knew what was happened. He was furious and beat me in front of police. Finally, police separated us and let my father take me home. They told my father that please do not beat your son at home, otherwise they will arrest us.

We went home. My father did not beat me. He took off his uniform and put it on my shoulders. I cried. From now on, every month, he bought a monthly pass for me and let me wear his uniform to go outside. That is not my dream. I need a place to show my talent.

44

My Husband and I First Pleasure

The Royal Agricultural Winter fair 2015 kicked off. My husband and I went there. In a boutique called "Running Wolf," they sell all kinds of materials about horses. My husband told me when he was young, his father often whipped him with a horse whip. When his father died, he threw the whip away. It is a pity. I did not see it. So I went to boutique and bought a whip for 56 dollars, not cheap.

I was excited and never that excited! On the way home, we talked about domestic discipline. I felt that I was just like a kid who was told to be punished at home. I expected it intensively and was shy. My whole brain focused on the whip and the lovely night. Yet we went home; I took a shower; my husband said that he did not want to do it today. My heart fell down to the bottom. Yet I had no choice.

Monday, I had something to do in the morning. Coming home, it is 12 a clock. I cooked and we finished lunch. Spontaneously, I needed to be whipped. I cannot wait, not a minute. My husband handcuffed me first, in case I will use my hand to block the whip and then break my finger. I was nude in the bed, butt up. This is his first time to be a spanker. He did it fast and a little bit hard. But I can tolerate; since I had already joined the Toronto Spanking Club for years. I saw the pictures and videos. The first episode lasted less than 5 minutes. I could not handle it. I did not know that just 5 minutes felt like half an hour past. Then we started again. This time, I liked it and it lasted much longer. I was up my butt and firm it. If it is too hurt, I would turned my body a little bit. Suddenly, my husband stopped it. And he found some books from the bookshelf. He asked me which one I like most. I said that I did not like it at all. Our discipline began.

This time he just beat me one side of bump one time, I felt happy. It didn't hurt at all. I said that we can play the whole day! He laughed at me. After a while, I guess that he did not like this game anymore. He whipped me very hard and on the both sides at the same time. I yield. He did not care. He is the master now. My hands were handcuffed together, preventing me from doing anything. The best part I must say is the sensation. He touched my butt, and asked me why I loved this. I said that it is just like repenting in church. Corporal Punishment and Sex are obsessive for me. I need to overcome them. Yet if I did not taste it, how can I forget it or give them up. The last part spanking is just like before. He stopped it. And he opened my handcuffs. I went to the master room to see my butt in the mirror. All was very red. I massaged it, it is just swollen. I cannot believe it. I saw the online spanking pictures which are bleeding! I felt painful when I sat down.

Anyway, this is our first time domestic doing spanking. I do not think that this is the last one. The more will come.

45

Double Pleasure

Today is Wednesday, I begged my husband to whip me again. Finally, he accepted. Just like last time, I was undressed and handcuffed to the bed. My butt has many spots black and blue. That cannot stopped us. I stick my legs and butt up. My husband uses the whip to discipline me. He beats me here and there- painful. Sometimes, he beats my bruised parts, double pleasure and both of us are proud of it. He is an amateur. I did not felt the peak. Also I am too timid to say "harder and deeper." With his whipping, I feel released and enjoyable. I do not get any abuse. I never say that I cannot take it anymore. I always want more; just like a kid always wants more candies. My husband now feels how his father felt when he beat him. He becomes a "daddy" now! (We have no children.)

Sometimes, it is very sore. I like it. I am not sick. I knew that a lot of people like it too but just cannot speak about it publicly. Finally, I beg him a dozen more, he refused. I touch my butt. It is hot. And he is too gentle. It is not brutal.

46

Birthday Gift

Today is my real birthday (November 23rd, 1975). My official birthday is July 23rd, 1975. Instead of playing patty cake, I let my husband whip me again. I am not joking; I need it. Before we did it, I recalled my life. I did do something wrong. I used TTC transfers I found; I shortchanged supermarket money. I had many times to hook up different men before we married. They said that "My womb is extremely tight." They could not make love with me. Anyway I deserve to be whipped.

My husband held the whip upstairs. I felt shy. He asked me, "Do you want to take off clothes." I said yes. I just took a shower and bare butt with a skirt. I took off the skirt nude in the bed. He handcuffed me. I love my husband; he loves me too. He whipped me not that brutally. At the beginning, he beat me left side and right side. It is fast though. I extremely firmed my ass. Then he became harder and deeper, I still can tolerate it. He often asked me how is felt and could he stop it. I said no; I want more. Sometimes I felt I did not have choice; it should happen and leave a mark for me or say a lesson. My husband beat me much painfully now. He said that "Lisa, it is swelling now, can you feel?" I said that "Sorry miss." He beat me more. He sometimes touched my butt. I asked him "what time is it?" He said 10 minutes to 12: 30 pm. I said that another 10 minutes more. He beat me very hard. I felt pain in ass. Thank God! Police did not come and arrest us. At the end, my butt bruised. He opened the handcuff. I said that, "thank you." I went to the master room, my husband held a mirror and let me see it. It scarlet red and bruised. But it still had many light spots. I went to bed. I had bed sore. My husband accompanied me in bed. I felt better.

I learnt my lesson. I would not do these bad things anymore. I want to be a good person. That is my best birthday gift.

47

Wheel Chair Transfer

If you were born in Canada, you won't feel that the wheel chair transfer is so special. It began in 1995. But for me, it saved my husband and my lives.

My husband got cancer in 2014. He needed to go to Toronto Cancer Hospital a lot of times. He was very sick and could not take regular TTC services, and I could not drive either. At this crucial time, first we found the hospital volunteer drive, yet sometimes they did not have services available; we took a Taxi which cost us some money. We almost could not afford it. My friend let us apply for wheel chair transfer. Fortunately, we passed the interview and enjoy this service. Since, he is a senior we just paid 2 dollars then we will go to the hospital or visit friends etc. I am an immigrant from P. R. of China. This kind of service is never heard of in China.

Very coincidently, my mother had ovarian cancer in China in 2015. I am the only child in my family in the meanwhile I took care of my ill husband in Canada. I could not come back to China at this time. My father sometimes asks my relatives to drive my mother to hospital; sometimes he calls a Taxi. In China now the Taxi is very expensive and hard to find. Also in China, you live in hospital which is not free. You need sums of money. My father almost cannot afford it! Also there is no free care giver in China; my father and my relatives take care of my mom in turn. They all over 60 years old; my father is 70 years old! I felt very hurt. On the other hand, I feel that I am very lucky to be living in Canada.

I wish that all of us should cherish our life now and be proud of it. Life is easier in Canada than in other place else. God bless Canada.

48

I am Sorry

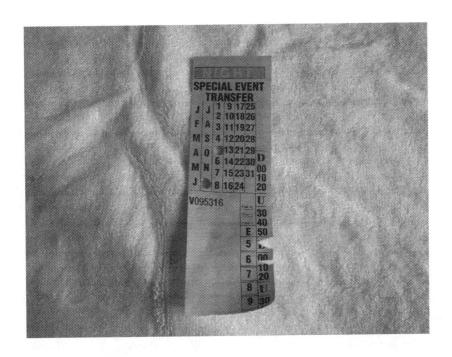

My parent call me Dear since I was young. I like this lovely and pretty name. Yet, for some students and teachers they called me Rudolph the red-nosed reindeer. Yes, I am. I had a tragic childhood. I was raised in a single mother's family. My father is a TTC driver. He has his own wife and child.

Anyway, everything passed. Now my father is almost retirement age. I have still no job. Last week, Toronto TTC hires and trains. My father asked his supervisor to give me a chance. Dear has mental illness for being bullied for years. But I often need to learn to know some knowledge about how to examine tickets. The first day of training, I was the No. 1. Everybody treated me seriously. Some called me fast bastard. I do not care. The second day, my trainer taught me how to drive street cars. I take medicine every day, so my reaction is slower than other normal persons. I forgot to change rails many times. My trainer felt very upset, because I may damage street cars and passengers. To be surprised, one of trainees screamed to me "*bus, bus.*" Firstly, I thought that he was suggesting I should drive a bus, yet one person told me secretly, "Bus means papa died" I immediately felt angry and was insulted. I found that person and slapped his face. When I was young some boys did the same thing to me. I was quite sad. That man called the police! The police came with a car and asked me whether I slapped him or not. I was calm and said yes. The police arrested me. They drove me to the police station and wrote down the confession. I was in the cell.

In the subway station, someone told my father that I was arrested. He was very worried about me. He found his manager, and pleaded for him to help me. The manager has worked with my father in decades. He said that, "It is emergency, we will drive my TTC official car there." My father said that "May I drive for you?" The manager said ok. They went to the police station. The manager explained the situation and wished that the police could let the TTC solve this problem. The police heard the story; they sympathized with me and tried to finish this case. I also felt very sorry for my father. I said that, "Dad, I am sorry." My dad cries. Police fingerprinted me and said that "Tomorrow, it is court day. You can leave after the bail hearing or if totally innocent can go home."

I said thank you to police and stay in my cell. My father and the manager left. I recalled my history, I feel sore. I wish that one day I can be a real man, and work in my strongest field.

49

To My Husband George

George and I met in Improve Place Saint Patrick's dance in 2013. We fell in love on the first sight. That night, together we took the subway back to our own home. Then we called each other often. I even helped him adopt a cat. He had an old cat "Harry" who was named after George's father.

One day, he invited me to his home. I liked the neighbour, so quiet and friendly. He even introduced me to his neighbours. Also he ask me, "Could you marry me?" Then he give me his grandpa's wedding ring as an engagement ring. That day, it is my first time living in his house. Soon we lived together. I let him join our church. He likes it very much. At the beginning, we had just a landlord and tenant relationship. He is very funny and witty. I like him. He also likes me sometimes to help him to do house work. After one year, we married in church.

George was a copyboy in Toronto Star from 19 years old to 21 years old. That is his best job and happiest one. George had a dream to be a social worker. He graduated from Humber School with a social worker major. But he did not find the professional job so he finally became a security guard. He had worked in security field for 25 years. He worked as a security officer at the biggest chocolate factory for 22 years. That was a miserable life. He as a night guard needed to go to the roof to check every night. It was very dangerous; also he carried a radio so the supervisor knew where he was. People gave him a nickname Raccoon. George is generous. He often gave gifts to his friends. He gave to big Helen a leather purse which was made himself. Once a supervisor retired, every security guard gave him a present. My husband made a pure leather wallet to him. He was very appreciative. The new supervisor said that: "From now on, no matter who leaves, just let George make a gift and everybody pays their portion."

George had a good friend who taught him how to do leather work. In our home, we have a lot leather tools and all kinds of stamps. Some are very rare. His father even made some unique tools for him to make leather work. Unfortunately, his friend passed away. He has not done leather work for years. George always say, "I miss him more than my father." Yes George is a good son. He took care of his parents and served them until they died. At that time, he was already 44 years old. So he was a single till he met me.

George' father and mother bought this house before he was born. And he lived in this house for life. He loves his house and revolution it twice. I as his wife take care of him as much as possible. We are the happiest couple.

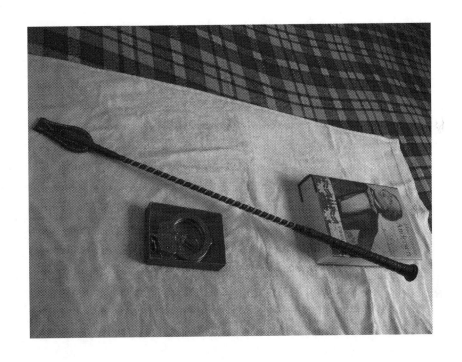

50

Toronto Rockyview Hospital the 9th Floor

December 11, 2015 I went to Toronto Rockyview Hospital (TRH) the 9th floor to see my psychiatrist. I came very early just like before. I was a little bit sleepy and closed my eyes while waiting my turn. People who wear leather shoes made big noises, which waked me up many times and I could not tolerate it anymore.

I opened my eyes to watch who did it. Firstly a psychologist whose name is Joanna Zhao often comes in and out and slams the door. Her high heel shoes also made me sick. Sometimes, she did not close the door; I saw her play the games on the computer! The patients told me that she took bribes yet her art of healing is minimal. No one likes her. When I said that: "you should be quiet." She poked and swore at me. It was not professional at all.

Another big noise maker is Dr. Leslie Buckleye. She is clinical head of Addiction service. She has a fair shawl. She is a very dangerous one. Once, she went to the nurse station and put some addiction drug to somebody's injection drug. It made that person lame. That is her laboratory dumb. Another time, she tried to do the same thing, yet the nurse was in the room, she was very nervous. She pretended to be calm and went back to her office; opened a bag of blue berry and came back to the nurse office to give some to the nurse. However, the nurse did not accept it. Her biggest hobby is coming late and going early.

Additions port. Mental Health wear a pair of black shoes that made noise which you cannot image! She is insolent. Within 5 minutes, she passed me over 6 times. Dr. Laeticia Eide of Community Mental Health is a young miss. She is the only one who wears a pretty watch and noisy shoes. But where are her patients? I did not see any. No patients' doctor is in TRH. Where is the money she got?

After the appointment with my psychiatrist. I went home and wrote down what I got from patients and practitioners. I still feel TRH is good, because the rest people are working hard and urbane. They are against the dark side for years. Our leaders should examine these as they are obviously true and let our hospitals be safe and reliable.

Printed in the United States
By Bookmasters